T0120622

Heroin Dreams

A young boy loving the paraphernalia
of the Lifestyle The Beginning

IamKnowOne

authorHOUSE®

AuthorHouse™
1663 Liberty Drive
Bloomington, IN 47403
www.authorhouse.com
Phone: 833-262-8899

Published by AuthorHouse 12/17/2020

ISBN: 978-1-6655-1105-6 (sc)
ISBN: 978-1-6655-1106-3 (e)

Library of Congress Control Number: 2020924871

Print information available on the last page.

This book is printed on acid-free paper.

Shots, shots, shots Firing and it sounds like Multiple Guns.

But the dude who schooled me, said none of us Runs.

I was taught to Stop and Listen, than I learned how to Judge the size of the Gun.

Small Pop Big Bang Automatic or Pump.

I could tell by the sound, who was real and who came to Front.

Pop pop pop, sounds like a fire cracker, it has to be a 22 revolver, that dummy just wanted to Stunt.

I started being a runner at the age of Eleven, every three hours I was given Two Grand and was told to put it Away.

Yup about every three hours, the guys had the projects lit, every single Day.

I never lost a dime, and was never Paid but remained Loyal every single Day.

As a young boy seeing that much money pass through my hands, made me a product of my Environment I must Say.

I kept observing, always learning and watching my Surrounding.

My Loyalty helped me gain respect, although I didn't have any money.

Their money was looking Resounding.

Growing up in the Hood is a Constant Struggle, what do we do, which way do we Go.

Yeah getting a college degree sounds good, but we didn't have Doctors or Lawyers around here to look up to, just Blow.

Most young Boys grow up in a single parent household, without a Father looking for Direction.

Looking up to Neighborhood Hustlers with Fast Money, Power and Dreaming that one day they'll make the Connection.

Hoping that an OG will take you under his Wing

And learning that one day you might have to kill a King, to become the King.

You're not thinking about a better Education for Money, that's not what you see by Far.

You're thinking about Fast Money, Women and Cars.

And in Your adolescent mind, this Life looks Amazing to you, Hell with the Laws.

At that very moment Heroin Dreams begin for Me.

As a Product of My Environment, a College Degree I couldn't See.

I was an eleven year old Baltimorean, Full of life with a Hustlers Ambition.

Walking through the projects with my A1 Damoe, we were always on a Mission.

BANG BANG BANG, sounds like A Glock 40, we didn't know it but over in the next court, my homeboys life had come to an End.

Blood Everywhere, one in the Head one in the body and two in the Chest.

Damn my Friends body was already laid to Rest.

He was only 13, never driven a Car and Never been with a Girl.

He was robbed and Killed, just a runner with so much Potential.

He could've been anything he wanted, instead of a Heroin runner in this World.

It was the day of the Funeral, My Homeboys Mom was a Heroin Addict.

She was Fading in and out during the whole funeral, crying of course and looking for a fix, although she knew she couldn't have It.

After the funeral, a few hustlers put up money for a block Party.

The media always makes it seem like hustlers are the worst species on the Planet.

But some of these kids moms and dads are junkies, in it's the hustlers, that make sure they're not Manic.

At the party we had a DJ, free food, entertainment, dancing and a lot of Girls.

No negative energy tonight, no guns, no fights everyone's Happy when females Twirl.

Damn I can't believe it, he was only 13 and now he's Dead.

I'm certain from this Day on I will forever be Messed up in the Head.

I realized that from now on, I wouldn't feel comfortable without a Gun.

But I'm only 11 with no positive role models to look up to and I can't Help thinking, is this how I'll raise my own Son?

Reminiscing

Walking and thinking, at the age of 7 I ran in the house crying and told my mom this kid had punched me in the Eye.

My Dad was never around, so my Mom was My tough Guy.

She stared at me with the look of death and said, go the Fuck back outside Now and Whip his Ass, Never Cry.

She literally pushed me back outside and locked the Door.

To you this might be abusive, where I'm From this was Survival and nothing More.

Long story short I ended up knocking on his Door.

I didn't know that my mom was in the window watching, she repeated something I said during the Fight.

She repeated, I got you now Bitch, what are you watching on TV at Night.

So we laughed together as she gave me some ice for my Eye.

I suddenly got a feeling of never wanting to be Apart.

But what I didn't know, was from that day on, Bravery would Always be in my Heart.

My mom said, you never know how tough you are until you get punched in the Face

I know you're only 7 but as you get older, you'll learn that these are words that you'll always Embrace

The Dome

Baltimore's Madison Square Garden

The Home of Midnight Madness

I still can't believe my homeboy lost his life, but I have to get my mind Right.

The Championship game is Tonight.

My second time playing under the Dome.

All of the Baltimore Legends played there, including Skip Wise, Muggsy Bogues, Kurk Lee and Sam Cassell

Eden and Biddle St. will be full of Hustlers Dope Cars and Fly Girls, I just hope I can Play Well.

And that wasn't to hard if you listened to Coach, because all he would say was, JUST GET THE BALL TO THE DIPPER.

Who was Skip Wise son, the Boy had Game and he could damn sure get it Done.

A lot of dudes from Baltimore City had and still have mad Game.

It's just these street temptations, fast money cars and gorgeous women that'll drive you Insane.

We ended up losing under the Dome to a team from West Baltimore, Bentalou by about 3 on that Court.

East and West Baltimore never really got along, but was respectful when it came to Sports.

As I walked through the crowd on my way home, observing the hustlers, wishing I had the cars and the Girls

And seeing this in the hood daily, was just Solidifying that I need this in my World.

BANG BANG 2 Shots Fired from a Big Ass Gun Sounds like a 45, than I hear Y'all know What Time it is, as everybody start to Run...

There was a dice game going on after the basketball game let Out.

2 Shots Fired from a 45 and that made everybody spread Out.

There's always a lot of Money and Blood shed involved during a dice Game.

But these dudes here, they don't know who the Fuck they just robbed because those niggas there, yeah they're Insane.

Dead men walking, they might as well have shot their own mom in the Brain.

Back than dudes were honorable, they lived by a Code.

To many women and kids were around after the Game to Retaliate, be smart not Bold.

So they'll wait and make moves in the shadows, and them dudes will most certainly Fold.

That next day we heard all three of the guys involved in the robbery was shot multiple times and Killed.

After two of their girlfriend's was kidnapped and their places of residence was Revealed.

Yeah these Baltimore Streets are for Real.

My cousin had just pulled a very important lick and asked me to hold the Gun.

And made it Very clear what to do if the police Come.

Back than certain guns were harder to get in the Hood.

So we kept them close until we was sure the heat was on and that had to be Understood.

It was Never a thought, what that gun could have possibly been used For.

All I knew was to Remain Loyal and nothing More.

1200 Elm leaf Ct.

Knock Knock Knock, Damn the Fucking Police is at the Door.

And I got this Big ass Gun, my mom is going to kill me, FUCK.

I have to try and hide this under the Floor.

My mom opens the door but they're looking for her boyfriend, they said he was involved in an armed Robbery.

Damn I thought someone was snitching, thank goodness, but he's always involved in some type of Debauchery.

After they ask moms a few questions they were on their Way.

I was very Relieved, but I hoped my moms was going to be Ok.

KNOCK KNOCK KNOCK, two hours later Sounds like Someone is Breaking the Damn Door Down.

It was my cousin, outside with his face Full of Blood from a Police Beat Down.

Someone shot at a Cop and ran, and because my cousin was running during that Time.

Of Course he was a person of interest, but he was listening to his Walkman so he couldn't hear or see the Police from Behind.

They didn't give a Fuck, he was a young Black man running through Somerset Projects, and someone was going to Pay.

The cops said he was a known Drug Dealer, so I guess they figured that they would make an example out of him that Day.

I heard my mom screaming and crying, get the fuck off of my Nephew.

Than I heard the cop say, go back in the house Bitch there's nothing you can Do.

It took everything in me not to go outside with that Big ass Gun.

It's three cops beating on my cousin and one of you cowards called my mom a Bitch, but I knew that I would get no where being Dumb.

The Police really tried to Fuck my Cousin up, he was Beat down for something he didn't Do.

What happened to innocent until Proven guilty, not in the hood, most Police treat you as if they Own You.

And as a kid you start to think, is Police Brutality normal towards young Black Men?

Most Police looked at All of us in the Hood as if We didn't have a Chance in Hell to Win.

Just hoping my cousin gets better, he's a tough Guy.

But that Police Brutality Shit, that Can't continue to Fly.

I was still very relieved, that they wasn't coming for the Gun.

Nevertheless it was Certainly Fucked up what they've Done.

My cousin was back to the streets in a couple of Days.

Money can't make itself, was his favorite Phrase.

Shots Burst out BBBBBANG BBBBBANG that sounds suppressed but still Loud like a Mother Fucking MP5.

These Stupid ass Dudes come around the corner pull up to Lindenleaf Ct. and started spraying at everyone Outside.

Some people hit the ground, some started running and hiding, whatever was needed to stay Alive.

Good thing is most dudes in the hood couldn't shoot or Aim.

They Never tried to learn, they just Felt empowered by holding a Gun which was kind of Insane.

One of the runners recognized the guy holding the Gun.

He just killed him self, he might as well sit on a pair of 12 inch scissors his life is Done.

So Makaveli instructed the guys to load up the guns, including two Ak-47s and an RPK.

Them dudes probably don't even know, one of the bullets hit a 5 year old girl, her name was Nay

She was my home boys daughter,

Niggas in the Hood always took care of their Own.

But shooting while kids are playing in the middle of the day, that Shit will Never be OK.

Makaveli was young, fearless and ruthless, he loved his hood and did his best to make sure that we all stayed ten toes Down.

Everybody was Furious, and there was no way in Hell that we could calm my home boy Down.

Tonight will forever be a night to remember, because some of them dudes will unquestionably lie Down.

It's about 9:30 pm still around 70 degrees, with a light breeze Blowing.

They loaded up in 3 cars, everyone was instructed to take separate ways incase the Police lights start Glowing.

They all arrive at the location, there he go, they watch to see what the shooter is going to Do.

They send young runners to observe the situation, they give the sign Poo pooooo.

Everyone jump out of the cars and knew exactly what to Do.

The whole team started shooting, you heard a lot of guys scream in pain that Day.

Ahhh I'm Hit I'm Hit, but instructions was to keep Shooting.

Because this Shit here is personal and for Little Nay.

After Nay died, we damn sure made it Storm.

We know that whatever we did couldn't bring her back, but we wanted to make sure that all of them Mother Fuckers wish that they wasn't Born.

I was just a little nigga at the time, but I knew that my homeboy would always be Torn.

It was about a month later and no one could talk about Nay without our eyes tearing Up.

Than jordache had just came out and we were noticing girls with Big Butts.

I was gaining more skills and was being introduced to the ingredients to cut the Heroin.

Which could turn 300 dollars into 3000 dollars, depending on the amount of cut you put In.

The OG that taught me said, you got one time to do this shit the right Way.

If you fuck up our money, it will be hard for you to live another Day.

I was always a smart kid and I knew how to play my Position.

And I never fucked up because I didn't want to come up Missing.

There was so many fucked up things going on within those project Walls.

We wasn't living we was surviving, and when teenage girls came to you sharing personal information

You knew you had to stand Tall.

My homeboys little cousin had started taking an interest in Me.

And honestly she had a cute face, but that little booty was all I could See.

My homeboy told me to keep my head in the game and off of his little cousin before he fucked me Up.

But every time she came around my teenage dick got hard so I didn't give a Fuck.

But as we started getting closer, she told me that her uncle had been molesting her since age Eleven.

And she wished that someone would just shoot him and his dick, because that would surely teach him a Lesson.

Her mother was a single parent raising five kids on her Own.

She worked two jobs and thought she could trust her brother to stay with the kids, instead of leaving them Alone.

She described the first time that he touched her in a very meticulous Way.

It made my stomach hurt so bad, I couldn't even finish what I wanted to Say.

But I knew that molesting ass child fucker had to Pay.

I felt certain that this wasn't his first time touching a child, but I could damn sure try my best to make it his Last.

My homeboy said his grandfather use to say, the only way that a man would know how it feels to get raped,

Is to repeatedly stick something up his Ass.

It was about 7:30pm a breezy June evening and four dudes pulled up in a green Nissan Datsun 210.

The windows was slightly tinted, and they were driving to mother fucking slow.

All I heard was my cousin Scream, GET THE FUCK DOWN.

Damn I guess the Summer was officially about to Begin.

As soon as it gets warm in the Hood

That's when niggas start doing the most, and they're definitely up to no Good.

My cousin had just won his court case, he was accused of shooting at a Policemen.

He had to chill from the Streets until his case came to an End.

Shit they fucked his face up so Bad his lawyer told him to stay in school and don't worry, he guarantees a Win.

But while my cousin was gone, he had no idea of how much work that I was putting In.

My homeboy recognized one of the guys from the drive By.

So later, we was going to see if we could make him go Bye Bye.

Damn there goes my girlfriends uncle, well she's not really my Girl.

It's about 10pm now, I'm going to follow him and see if I can fuck up his World.

I told a few of my homeboys to walk with me, than told them that I've been having a problem with this Man.

So my homeboy put a blue nine millimeter to his head, just told him to walk and asked did he Understand.

So as we walked over to the Middle, that was what we called the middle school that we all went to in the Neighborhood.

Around the back of the school was about thirty steps that lead to the basement, with a long cafeteria table outside, so we could really tie him up Good.

We made him strip, than lay down on his stomach as we tied him Up.

I was thinking what my homeboy grandfather said, but I really didn't want to stick anything up his Butt.

One of my homeboys ran up the steps to see if he could find a tree branch or a Pole.

He ran into the OG when he reached the Top.

OG asked what the hell was we doing down there and that Honeycomb hideout Spot.

So my homeboy told, than OG approached me and asked me the Story.

I told him that his little cousin had been getting molested by their uncle for years and was afraid to tell her Story.

He asked me if I believed the story was absolutely True.

I said definitely, than he sent my homeboy back over to the projects to get cockeyed Doug.

AH shit that nigga is a Super Thug.

Cockeyed Doug was about six feet three inches tall weighed about 325 pounds, only 21 years old and was known for Murders.

OG said when he get here, you little niggas need to go.

So when he got there we acted like we left, than we heard OG ask did you hurt Her.

Well of course he lied and said No.

Than we heard cockeyed Doug say thanks, now I'm going to fuck the truth out of you real slow and make you my Hoe.

Obviously we didn't believe it until we heard her uncle start to Scream.

Damn he was really getting it, so we ran as fast as we could,

I just remembered saying Damn I wish that was a Dream.

I would have never thought an Alpha Thug like that would have ever thought about penetrating another man.

Damn Damn Damn.

Damn that nigga had his own uncle Fucked.

I know I ain't never fucking up the Cut.

He obviously deserved it, fucking with little girls that sick ass bastard ain't Shit.

And now I know he'll be thinking about what the fuck he did every time he takes a Shit.

Now I need to think of a way that I can increase this Money.

So I can stay on OG's good side, because I like girls to much to become another mans Honey.

You got to learn how to become a good soldier before you can move up in Rank.

So I just played my position stayed focused on my surroundings, so I could always Think.

Damoe and I played a lot of basketball growing up, we would play in different hoods and there was always some Mess.

We had an outside game against a team named Cecil Kirk but it was over West.

While I should have been focusing on the game, I saw this junkie that I served plenty of Drugs.

So I asked Coach could I use the restroom, than walked over to him to see what it Was.

Sho Nuff it was Heroin, so I asked him why was he all the way across town buying, instead of buying from Us.

He said that their shit was a lot better, more potent and our shit compared to there's was a Bust.

The Cut 5:1

Than I started to think, I remembered we mixed seven scoops of powder per one gram of Heroin.

See the Cut, that's how the Money comes In.

So I told OG that the junkie said that the Boy

over West shoots more Pure.

And if we don't change something soon, than more junkies would start going over West for Sure.

So on our next Re Up, let's try putting a five on it instead of a Seven, OG said that sounds like a Plan.

That's why I Fucks with you, my little Man.

So I said do you Fuck with me enough let me feel your cousins Butt.

OG said, Boy don't make me Fuck You Up.

Than he told my cousin to make sure that the process happens, and don't be trying to Stunt.

In the meantime take me to Charlie Rudo and get me a pair of the new Air Force ones or whatever I Want.

As we were on our way to Old Town Mall, We saw my mom Crying.

My uncle had hit a women in the head with the back of an axe, and she might be Dying.

My uncle had just got out of jail about a month Ago, he use to love to Connive.

He bought a soda and a whatchamacallit, he gave her a twenty dollar bill but she gave him change for a Five.

Again he told her that he gave her a twenty. she argued no and said Five

So he walked next door to the hardware store bought an axe, hit the women in the head than waited for the police to Arrive.

Damn Unc, Really and a Woman

I'm going back over to the Projects, I hear the police Coming.

The police came and took my Unc Away.

My moms kept crying, but she knew he was wrong and there was nothing that she could Say.

But now it's time to Re Up, time to decrease the Cut.

So we can get this Fucking Money Up.

Damn there goes my girl, well Again she's not my girl Yet.

But she got them fucking Chic jeans on, and I know they're her moms but I'm sure she got one of the biggest asses in Somerset.

A Yooo.. hold up for minute what's going on, you're looking very pretty today just like a little dream Doll.

I'm good I'm about to catch the Five bus and meet the girls at Mondawmin Mall.

Ok be careful, you know niggas get crazy up There.

But for you, I'll smack a niggas momma like I don't Care.

Just joking have Fun.

About five minutes after she walked away I here BBBBANG BBBBANG, some dude than came around here shooting this big ass Gun.

Sounds like a Desert eagle 50 cal, if that shit hit someone, I guarantee you that they're no longer Alive.

Let's check on the crew and make sure no one took a Dive.

The boys and I have to walk up the street to see what's going On.

Shit that was my cousin showing off, fucking with OG and the boy Don.

So we walked to the stash house to cut up the Dope.

And see cockeyed Doug, beating up a dude tied to a Rope.

Damn this nigga got men sex Slaves

I'll make sure I stay away from this dude, before one of us end up in the Grave.

So I asked OG should we do this here, or go out Cherry Hill to the other House.

OG said nah, make up them fucking Jumbos here, we're good this my House

This was the dude that tried to rob your cousin, so until y'all finish that lil Bitch will be as quite as a Mouse.

So after we finished, we treated it as if it was new product, so we had to give out Testers.

HITTING IN THE WHOLE, Everybody line the fuck up and follow the dude with the ugly ass Sweater.

The same dude I saw buying over west tested it Out.

Than said this shit right here nigga is what a dope fiends life should be About.

Hearing that felt so fucking Good.

Our lives was about to change, as it fucking Should.

Everything was looking Gravy, we started making more money and increased the Team.

OG started sending my cousin on licks, he couldn't tell me what was going on, but sometimes it was days before he was Seen.

We had tickets to the RUN DMC Concert that Saturday night.

OG said make sure that everybody Strap up, stay close and always make sure that everyone is Alright.

The Concert was Dope as Fuck, Who's House.. RUNS House.. stayed in my head for Days.

But who else Rock the house, none other than Public Enemy and that Mother Fucking FLAVA FLAV...

Of course the S1W's was on Deck

And FLAV had that big ass clock, Chilling around his Neck.

After the concert, there was always fighting shooting, robbing and putting niggas to Sleep.

Murphy Homes was Famous for traveling with at least twenty to Fifty Deep.

We lived within walking distance of the Baltimore Civic Center.

So as we walked home, Gun shots started BBBRANG. BBBRANG sounded like a Forty-five was going to be the Experimenter.

OG said Stop why the Fuck are you running, Never run just because you hear gun Shots Yo.

Especially when You don't even know where they're coming from, just get Low.

Than my cousin and my homeboy came around the corner with this Thick ass Gold rope Chain.

So at that moment I realized who was doing the shooting, and that we were into more than just selling Heroin and Cocaine.

My cousin was playing basketball with these dudes that he knew from Flag House Projects.

One of the dudes fouled him really hard and called him a Bitch.

My cousin was playing with that Gold chain on that he just acquired, and them Niggas was jealous of It.

Before my cousin could even get up from off of the ground.

Cockeyed Doug pulled out two pretty ass Tech Nines and said I wish any of you Niggas Ever think about trying It.

My cousin loved to Fight, I thought he was about to Fuck dude Up.

But he just walked over to dudes girl and said whenever you're ready to get rid of that lame, I'm in the first building on Exeter street sixth floor look me Up.

Them Niggas was Heated but they all heard stories about Cockeyed Doug.

They knew if anything Ever went down, and he had the opportunity, that he would enjoy making the next man his Love.

OG had just beeped my cousin, in the numbers 187 showed up in his Pager.

That meant strap the fuck up and get to a certain place right away Never Later.

But first we had to stop and get my cousin homeboy, he lives off of Calhoun and Baker.

C. B. S. was definitely three streets in the City that everybody knew About.

Don't ever attempt to walk through there looking like you don't belong or your Punk ass won't come Out.

He also contacted his homie Buddy from Lafayette projects, this nigga was a straight menace that everyone knew About.

Than he page his homie Killa from Latrobe, and told him if you see 187 in your pager, y'all niggas get ready to Roll.

All of us showed up at the location and was ready for Whatever.

OG said it's only been about three months since we increased the team and changed the cut, which was Clever.

Money is looking Great now, so to show my appreciation we have some fucking celebrating to Do.

So all of us went to El's Strip Club, O G said don't say shit about your age just stand tall and walk Through.

It was my young ass first time at a Strip Club and All of that Ass shaking was Unbelievable.

At that very moment Heroin Dreams, money, sexy women and chilling with my team was certainly Believable.

Damn I kept thinking about that Strip club all Night.

When I woke up I noticed that there was something in my bed that wasn't quite Right.

Shit I need to put on something fresh today, like my new Sergio Tacchini sweat suite, baby blue, black and White.

So I can fuck up somebody's daughter Eyesight.

It's the middle of July Friday about 7am, OG taught us to handle business as early as We Can.

He would always say the police are not looking for to much criminal activity that early Man.

So we would transport to our team first thing in the Morning.

The really good thing was that the traffic was always Boring.

Everything was done, now it's time to start my Day.

Like I said eyes will turn, it's time for the girls to look my Way.

It's a party tonight at my homeboy Yae Crib.

His mom gives the best waist line parties ya Dig.

And I was determined to lay up in something, fuck it she can take my Rib.

So we danced all night rocking to Baltimore's club music, Through that Dick.

Yae use to love to do that dance, but I was still a virgin, so that song was making me Sick.

Nevertheless I Finally got my girls number, so I felt like the man, so now you can't tell me Shit.

I had mad fun, Damn that House party was Lit.

As we leave out the party BBBRRATT BBBRRATT Gun shots ring out, sounds like a Tech.

Everyone starts to run, a car pulls off than I realize my homeboys sister got shot in the Neck.

My homeboy runs over and immediately starts to Cry.

Looking up at the sky asking God Why.

The ambulance came and took her to Johns Hopkins hospital for Care.

But my other friend saw the car, and it was them niggas from Flag House projects

We got em Oh Yeah.

My Homeboy's sister Died before she got to the Hospital.

That night I'm sure everyone cried far more than a Little.

At the time my cousin was living in Flag House Projects.

So he was cool with certain dudes, come to find out, the guys who did it was from an entirely different Set.

But because of what happened to my homeboys sister, we knew them niggas had to get Wet.

OG said it was time to make a Run.

He gave my Homeboy a Bag for his Family and told him to chill for a few days because he was damn sure Done.

We drove over West to Park Heights to meet up with OG's OG Big Shock.

He had a hook up on some guns that just touchdown at Baltimore's Dock.

Shock knew Everything about Everything that was coming into the City, not just the Drugs.

What is was, when and where it was arriving, the prices and the Plug.

OG told us that him and another dude put so much work in for Big Shock, that he treated them like his Sons.

OG said years ago Big Shocks Mom, sister and daughter was Kidnapped, tied up and locked in a closet because the dudes wanted Big Funds.

OG said that as soon as his OG found out, he went Fucking Nuts.

Somehow he found out where they were hiding his family at and only told my OG and a dude named Nut.

OG said you have to Really be sure who you trust these days, niggas will lie and Snitch.

Some dudes act like their the King Alpha but in the inside they're a weak little Bitch.

So OG and Nut suited up and handled the Work.

Them niggas wasn't expecting company so Nut kicked the door in, OG shot one in the chest and watch the 9mm bullet make the other dudes head Jerk.

They took OG's family and got out of there, when the Streets heard what happened they instantly knew that OG was the Man.

And my OG and Nut got respected throughout Murderland.

He told them both that they were now his sons until the day that he Dies, so they'll never Fail.

But somehow Nut got caught up with Kingpin and multiple Murder charges, than got life in Jail.

But by that time the Streets had to much Love for Nut riding with OG.

So even from jail Nut still controlled some of the major business going on in Baltimore City.

The guns that came in were thirty six Bushmaster AR 15s.

To have that many automatic weapons at one time was a Hood niggas Dream.

But OG said that he was doing a favor for his Homie Philly.

Than told us what he wanted done with the guns, and said don't get fucking Silly.

So we took the guns to a discrete location, an abandoned warehouse with a vault in the Basement.

We locked the guns in, than put the same three dudes on a twenty four hour watch no Replacements.

While they were watching the guns, we started looking for the niggas that killed my homeboys Sister.

We can't let that ride, we always take care of our own but right now it's a brain Twister.

So OG contacted Nut to see if there was talk of it within the jail Walls.

Nut said he asked his team, and no one heard anything at All.

Than OG told one of my homeboys to make a delivery to some dudes in Westport.

About three hours later we heard my homeboy was robbed and killed in broad daylight, right in the middle of the Court.

The Westport dudes reached out ASAP.

They said it was some Haitian niggas, that had beef with their boy Little P.

They said that both of them got shot trying to make the Transaction.

Little P was only hit in the shoulder, than ran off with the money and the product, thanks to his quick Reaction.

They told OG the product was secure but now it's time for some serious Action.

One of the dudes from Westport recognized one of the Haitians, he said his girl lives in Pioneer City, lets get Satisfaction.

Pioneer City is a Certified Hood in Anne Arundel County, MD that most people in Baltimore never heard of at All.

Them niggas out there most certainly handle their Fucking business, if you think they're just County friendly, you will get Mauled.

OG reached out to his man Bum beetles who had Family in Pioneer City.

He told OG that the Haitian dude seemed madly in love with a girl named Kitty.

So OG got the team together, reached out to Westport and Pioneer City and told them when the Shit was going Down.

Meanwhile OG's homeboy Philly had just Touchdown.

OG updated Philly on what he had going On.

So he left OG with three of the Bushmaster AR 15s and two bags of cash before moving On.

Tonight was the night everyone was in Place

It's about eleven pm, a cool breeze was blowing, when we kicked the door in, you couldn't believe the look on that motherfuckers Face.

Come to find out he wasn't even Haitian, when that bastard started screaming that accent started Fading.

OG didn't want him shot it was to personal, can you believe this Shit.

With all of the fire power we had including three AR 15s, he didn't want him Hit.

So he was Stabbed repeatedly over fifty times,

I was still a pre teen and never seen no shit like that in my Life.

But OG said that it was time for me to see how it feels, to have another mans blood on my hands, using only a Knife.

Anyone could use a gun but a Knife that shit is Personal.

In the look in their eyes when you stick that knife in, could never be Reversible.

I had nightmares for about a week Straight

Than I finally knocked on my girls door although it was really Late.

I think i just wanted someone beside me so I could Sleep.

But when I woke up she was kissing my Feet.

It took my mind off of my troubles momentarily, but now I have to live with my Reality.

The next day I got up and it's suppose to be business as usual, but OG house just got raided and I heard there was a Fatality.

After the stomach pains throwing up and telling myself that I'm not built for this Shit.

I got a call from OG and got myself together real Quick.

Deeee. (Moms calling)

Yes. You have a collect call from the Jail

It was OG, they gave him King Pin and murder charges no Bail.

He also shot the first two cops that came through his bedroom Door.

They wasn't in uniform, OG was a monster with a gun, but than he saw his girl laying dead on the Floor.

Our phone conversation was very brief, but through certain letters of certain words, I knew my next Move.

He wanted the cop that shot his girl dead, along with the three dudes that snitched, torched and abused

And I had to Approve.

He consulted me on who he wanted to do it, and when in where it could be Done

He always told me that he never had to worry about me, because he knows that I know how to live in the shadows, because IamKnowOne.

One of the dudes that snitched was his cousin, he didn't care it had to be Done.

He told me after it was done, to give his aunt enough money to pay for the funeral and to tell her that he would always be her second Son.

I also had to make sure that his wife and kids was always OK.

And to keep his wife from finding out that he even had a girlfriend, especially after his chargers that he received that Day.

Damn I'm still a teenager with So much on my mind, but I have to man up OG needs me Focused.

So I put out his orders before the police tried to approach Us.

Two of the dudes that snitched was supposed to get hit right Away.

One of them got hit right in front of his mom, OG wanted it that Way.

His cousin got Murdered in front of our entire Crew.

OG wanted to make him an example, if he would do that to his cousin, imagine what would happen to You.

Finally someone found out the niggas that killed my homeboys Sister.

Now the AR's could be used, but we were also instructed to kill the head dudes baby mother, and after she was dead the hitter was told to Kiss Her.

A kiss of her leaving this world that Night.

Make sure everyone knew not to Fuck with our crew, Because what they thought could be done in dark, would most certainly come to Light.

OG would always say project niggas live in Hell, because they only look up to the Streets.

Come to find out the first cop he shot, killed his girl, and although he felt somewhat Complete.

He said cops are never supposed to be marked, so never let your feelings end this Food that we all Eat.

The dudes that killed my homeboys sister, was on Alameda and Coldspring lane.

It wasn't there hood, but where they would usually Meet.

We had two stolen 5.0's, one black one red, four of us to a car, the AR holders was in the rear passenger Seat.

It was about 5pm, I remember it was a nice day, about seventy five degrees, the sun was shining but not much Heat.

There they go siting in a baby blue Rx7, with the baby blue BBS, damn that car was Sweat

We pull up on the side of the street, three cars back, the AR holders got out and walked up to each side of the Car.

BRAAAATTT..... BRAAAATTT.... BRAAAATTT...

They pulled their masked up after it was done, because they wanted them niggas to see their face, than back to the Cars.

One of the guys saw the head Dudes baby moms walking towards the car after the shooting, and Damn she's Pregnant.

We have to tell OG that it's done, but she can't get It.

He didn't give a fuck about killing women especially after so many of ours has fallen, but he always said even if you get a kid by mistake you're Cursed.

A few weeks later we found out that one of OG homeboys was fucking dudes baby mother, and that baby could possibly be his First.

OG knew the owner of the best strip club in the city, and told him that he was sending us down on a Monday when it wasn't real Busy.

He was trying to get us to chill for a bit, because he know that we had so much going On.

And from the way that we were living, one mistake and we were forever Gone.

I was the youngest of the crew, and again I didn't even have a fake ID

But during another phone conversation OG said you'll Always be good because you totally ride for Me.

My lil nigga, you've never been average, one of these days I'm fitting to make you an OG.

Fitting to make, I wanted to laugh bad, but not at OG.

OG you must not be from Baltimore, indeed I am, but the trap will always be the trap, no matter where you Be.

Just stay ten toes down, and only fuck with real niggas like Me.

After we got off of the phone, I knew that he wanted me to go down Flag House and holla at Cockeyed Doug.

The Super thug that liked to fuck Thugs.

I always did exactly what I was told and got the fuck away from Cockeyed Yo.

Real talk, that big nigga made me nervous, but I understood his position Though.

He was the first dude to call me a pimp and said that he like my Style.

He said that he heard that I had the girls around the projects going Wild.

The next day we had to pick him up for a job, than I saw my aunt come out of his House.

As she was leaving, she walked up to him and kissed him in the Mouth.

But he Fucks Men.. and my Aunt, damn I'm fucking confused WOW.

Printed in the United States
By Bookmasters